THE
CAT
AND THE
RAT
AND THE
HAT

First published 2021 by Nosy Crow Ltd, The Crow's Nest,
14 Baden Place, Crosby Row, London SE1 1YW
www.nosycrow.com

ISBN 978 1 83994 092 7 (HB)
ISBN 978 1 83994 156 6 (PB)

Nosy Crow and associated logos are trademarks and/or registered trademarks
of Nosy Crow Ltd.

Text © Em Lynas 2021
Illustrations © Matt Hunt 2021

A CIP catalogue record for this book is available from the British Library.

Printed in China
Papers used by Nosy Crow are made from wood grown in sustainable forests.

10 9 8 7 6 5 4 3 2 1 (HB)
10 9 8 7 6 5 4 3 2 1 (PB)

To Chris, Hannah
and baby Hettie.
Get reading!
Buy ALL the books!
E.L.

For Maxwell,
M.H.

EM LYNAS

MATT HUNT

THE
CAT
AND THE
RAT
AND THE
HAT

This is the **cat**
that sat on the **mat**

and played
on the **mat**

and slept
on the **mat**

and dreamt
on the **mat**.

And
this is
the **rat**
that had
a big **hat**.

And this is the cat
that sat on the mat
that saw the rat
that had a big hat

and said . . .

I WANT
THAT
HAT!

And this is the **cat** that chased the **rat**

that had a big hat all over the mat.

And this is the **cat** with the **hat**.

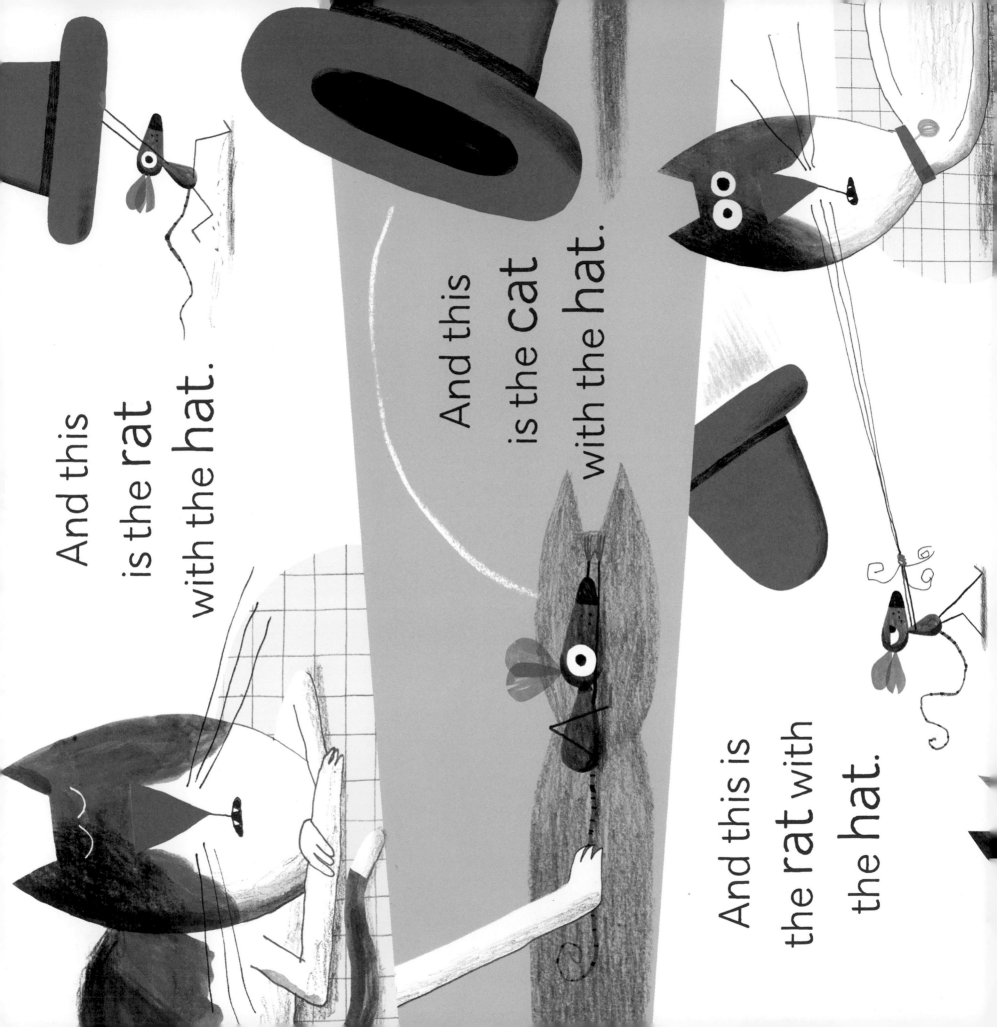

And this is the rat with the hat.

And this is the cat with the hat.

And this is the rat with the hat.

And this is the cat with the hat.

And this is the cat with the hat.

And this is the rat with the hat.

And this is
the cat
and
the rat
with the hat
on the mat.

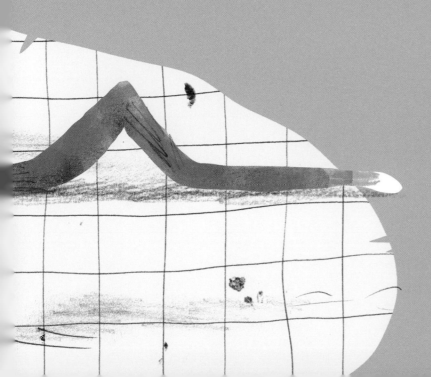

And this is the bat
with a fancy cravat
that saw the cat
and the rat
with the hat
on the mat
and said . . .

And this is the **bat** that twisted and twirled like an acrobat,

that flicked
and flapped
that fancy cravat
at the cat
and the rat
with the hat
on the mat.

And this is the cat and the rat that said . . .

I WANT THAT
FANCY CRAVAT!

And this is the **rat** that dashed and snatched the fancy **cravat**.

And this is the **cat** that sat on the **rat** with a **SPLAT!**

And this is the cat
with the fancy cravat.

And this is the rat
with the fancy cravat.

And this is the
cat with the
fancy cravat.

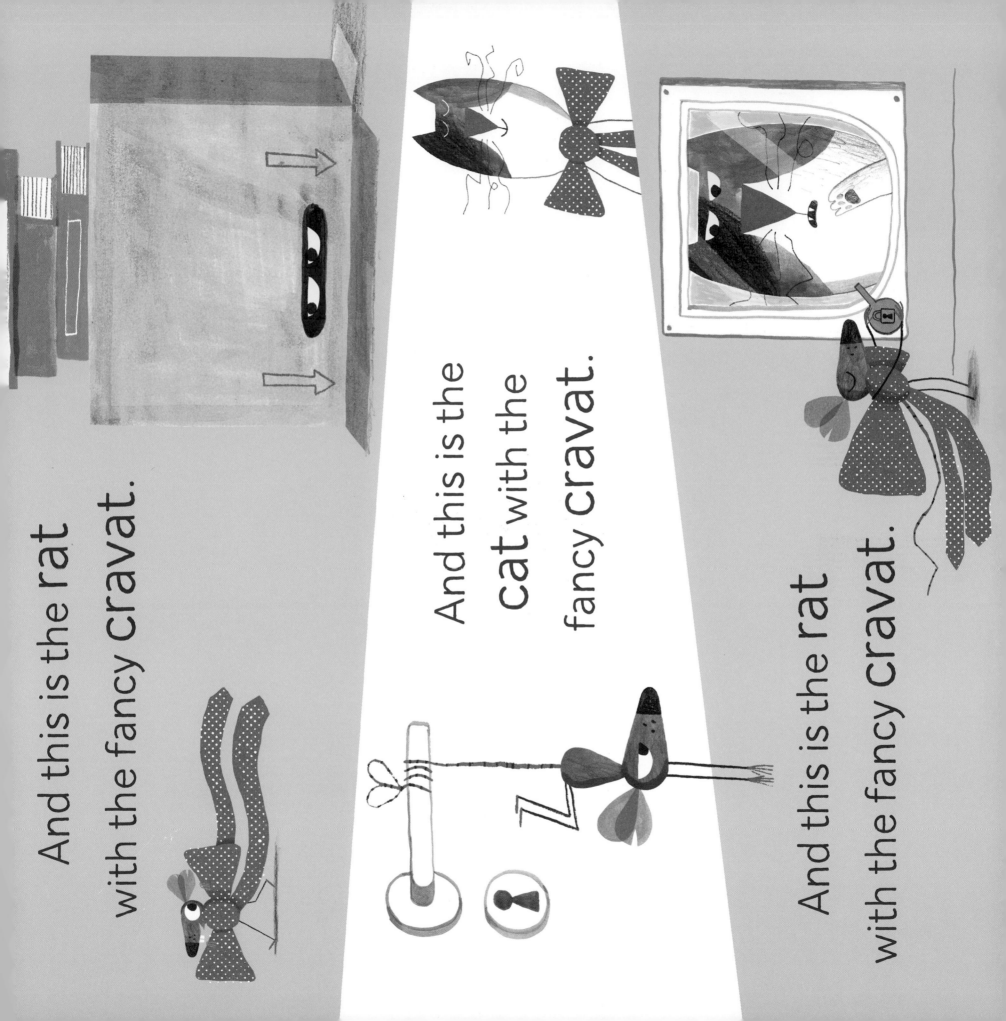

And this is the rat
with the fancy cravat.

And this is the
cat with the
fancy cravat.

And this is the rat
with the fancy cravat.

And this is the **bat**
that sat in the **hat**

and played
in the **hat**

and slept
in the **hat**

and dreamt
in the **hat**.

And this is the cat
and the rat
on the mat
with the fancy cravat
that said . . .

OH, DRAT! THE BAT GOT THE HAT!

And that is that.